Good Boy

Good

Boy

by Sergio  Ruzzier

 Atheneum Books for Young Readers
atheneum New York London Toronto Sydney New Delhi

ATHENEUM BOOKS FOR YOUNG READERS

An imprint of Simon & Schuster Children's Publishing Division

1230 Avenue of the Americas, New York, New York 10020

Copyright © 2019 by Sergio Ruzzier

ATHENEUM BOOKS FOR YOUNG READERS is a registered trademark of Simon & Schuster, Inc. Atheneum logo is a trademark of Simon & Schuster, Inc.

For information about special discounts for bulk purchases, please contact Simon & Schuster Special Sales at 1-866-506-1949 or business@simonandschuster.com.

The Simon & Schuster Speakers Bureau can bring authors to your live event. For more information or to book an event, contact the Simon & Schuster Speakers Bureau at 1-866-248-3049 or visit our website at www.simonspeakers.com.

Book design by Ann Bobco

The text for this book was set in Quimbly.

The illustrations for this book were rendered in ink and watercolor.

Manufactured in China

1118 SCP

First Edition

10 9 8 7 6 5 4 3 2 1

Library of Congress Cataloging-in-Publication Data

Names: Ruzzier, Sergio, 1966- author, illustrator.

Title: Good boy / Sergio Ruzzier.

Description: First edition. | New York : Atheneum Books for Young Readers, [2019] | Summary: Illustrations and simple text follow a boy and a dog on an out-of-this-world adventure.

Identifiers: LCCN 2018011052 (print) | LCCN 2018017938 (eBook) | ISBN 9781481499071 (eBook) | ISBN 9781481499064 (hardcover)

Subjects: | CYAC: Dogs—Fiction. | Adventure and adventurers—Fiction.

Classification: LCC PZ7.R9475 (eBook) | LCC PZ7.R9475 Goo 2019 (print) | DDC [E]—dc23

LC record available at https://lccn.loc.gov/2018011052

To R. W.

Sit.

Stay.

Roll over.

Stand.

Shake.

Bow.

Fetch.

Jump.

Juggle.

Cook.

Serve.

Eat.

Clean.

Come.

Pedal.

Fix.

Sail.

Build.

Speak.

Smile.

Home?

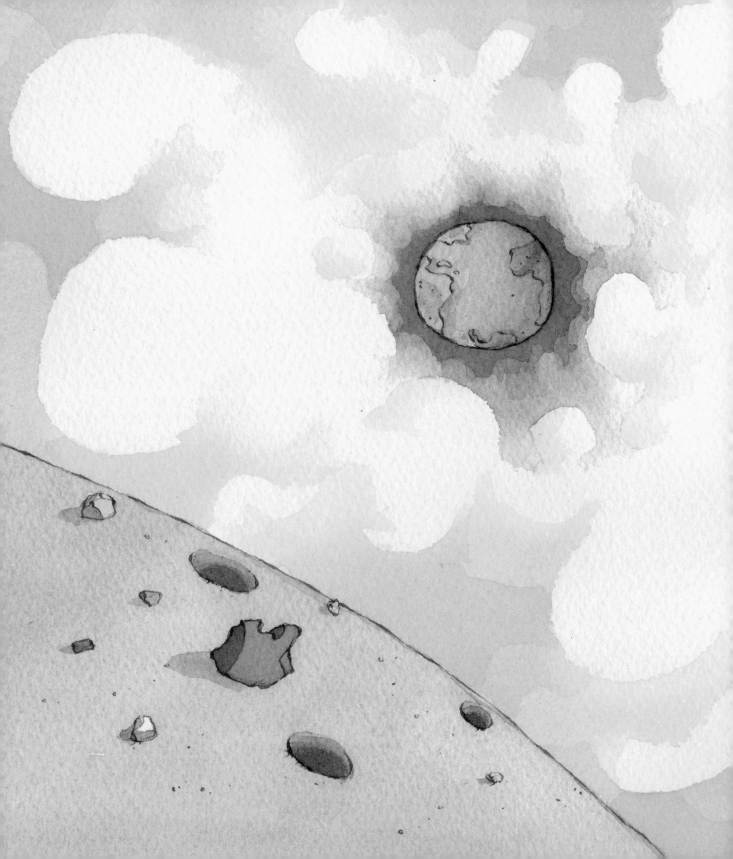

Home.

Wash.

Brush.

Dress.

Read.

Sing.

Stay.

Good boy.